R0083472688

P9-AOH-937

2015

Down at the Docks

A Random House PICTUREBACK® Book

Illustrated by Richard Courtney

Random House New York

Thomas the Tank Engine & Friends®

A BRITT ALLCROFT COMPANY PRODUCTION

Based on The Railway Series by The Reverend W Awdry. © 2003 Gullane (Thomas) LLC.
Thomas the Tank Engine & Friends and Thomas & Friends are trademarks of Gullane Entertainment Inc.
Thomas the Tank Engine & Friends is Reg. U.S. Pat. TM Off.

A HIT Entertainment Company
All rights reserved under International and Pan-American Copyright Conventions.
Published in the United States by Random House Children's Books, a division of Random House, Inc., New York,
and simultaneously in Canada by Random House of Canada Limited, Toronto.

www.randomhouse.com/kids/thomas   www.thomasthetankengine.com

Library of Congress Control Number: 2003001063

ISBN 0-375-82592-4 Printed in the United States of America First Edition 30 29 28 27 26 25 24 23

PICTUREBACK, RANDOM HOUSE and colophon, and PLEASE READ TO ME and colophon are registered trademarks of Random House, Inc.

Peeeeep! Everyone sure looks busy today, thought Thomas. He was on the hill overlooking the Brendam Docks. From above the busy harbor, Thomas could look down and see all of the other engines working hard.

"Maybe I can do something to help." And down he went.

When Thomas arrived at the docks, the other engines were bustling around. Everyone was working hard to prepare for the Ocean Life Exhibit, which was coming to the Island of Sodor. James and Cranky the Crane were busy unloading a big shipment of ocean plants. The plants would be put in the fish tanks to make the fish feel at home.

"Can I help?" asked
Thomas.
"Oh, little Thomas.
An engine like me
doesn't need help,"
said James.

Thomas chugged over to where Harvey was moving
a bunch of small crates.

"Keep back, little Thomas . . . these crates are full of
all the empty fish tanks and they are very fragile," said
Harvey. "We don't need you to be breaking anything."

As Thomas moved off, he noticed two cars coupled to Salty on the next track. He had never seen cars like this before. They were large and Thomas could see through their sides. They were full of water! A big octopus was swimming in the rear car. Thomas was amazed.

Then he pulled up to the front car. It had a huge shark in it.
The shark looked at Thomas and opened his mouth. He had rows
of big, scary teeth.

"Look at that!" Thomas gasped, and hurried up to find Salty.

"Amazin', aren't they, these critters from the deep? Eh, Thomas?" said Salty.

"Where are they from, Salty?" Thomas asked excitedly. "Where are they going?"

"They're off to an ocean show in Tidmouth. It sure is fun havin' 'em here, don't you think?" answered Salty with a smile.

I can't wait to tell Percy about them, thought Thomas. *Maybe we can see them in Tidmouth.*

Thomas was still marveling over the shark when Henry rushed by. "Out of the way. I am in a hurry," Henry whistled.

"Don't fret, Thomas," said Salty. "Little engines can be mighty handy at times."

"Thanks, Salty," peeped Thomas sadly. "Maybe there's something I can do back at the station."

Just as Thomas was leaving the docks, Percy came chugging up, working hard, pulling the afternoon mail.

"Percy, you've got to take a look at the cars that Salty is—" Thomas started.

"Not now, Thomas," Percy interrupted. "I need to deliver this mail right on time." And he hurried past.

Percy passed Salty and then looked up and saw . . .
a huge shark looking right at him!
"Yikes!" he tooted loudly, and rushed forward.

Percy was so surprised and so scared that he didn't look where he was going . . . Henry was stopped ahead of him on the same track. He was waiting for Harvey to cross with his fragile load.

Percy ran right into Henry, pushing him up the track . . .
right toward Harvey's cargo of fish tanks.

"Watch out, Harvey!" tooted Henry.

Harvey looked back, saw Henry rushing at him,
and went full steam ahead.
TOO LATE!

CRASH!

Henry crashed into Harvey's freight car!!

Harvey's freight car tipped off the track and the coupling snapped. Harvey, still at full steam, rushed forward.

He ran right into James. James was pushed off the track, which startled Cranky. Cranky let go of the crate he was carrying. The crate fell right onto James and burst, covering him with seaweed.

Thomas saw what happened and came hurrying back to help. His smaller size made it easy for him to fit between all the bumped engines and broken crates.

First, he helped pull Percy back on the track.